MW00669061

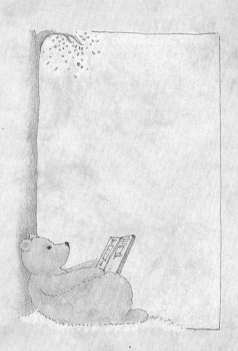

This book was first published in 1987 by Bracken Books
a division of Bestseller Publications Ltd
Princess House, 50 Eastcastle Street
London W1N 7AP, England

ISBN 1 85170 122 2

Printed and bound by Times Printers, Singapore

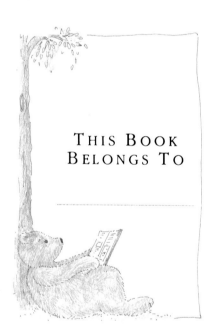

THIS BOOK
BELONGS TO

GOLDILOCKS
— AND THE —
THREE BEARS
And Other Tales

THE TWELVE DANCING PRINCESSES
FOX AND A CROW
HANSEL AND GRETEL
JACK THE GIANT-KILLER
BEAUTY AND THE BEAST
SNOW WHITE AND ROSE RED
THE TINDER BOX
THE THREE LITTLE PIGS
THE FROGS CHOOSE A KING

RETOLD BY
GERALDINE CARTER

ILLUSTRATED BY
JANE HARVEY

BRACKEN BOOKS
LONDON

Goldilocks and the Three Bears

Once upon a time there were three bears who lived in a house right in the middle of a wood. The first was a Little Tiny Baby Bear, the second was a Medium-sized Mummy Bear, and the third was a Great Big Daddy Bear. Each bear had his own porridge bowl; a small bowl for Little Tiny Bear, a standard bowl for Medium-sized Bear, and a large bowl for Great Big Bear. And each of them had a chair; a small chair for Little Tiny Bear, an ordinary chair for Medium-sized Bear

and a large chair for Great Big
Bear.

One breakfast time after
cooking porridge the bears
found that it was much too
hot. They decided to go
for a walk in the wood
while the porridge was
cooling down. As
they were playing in
the woods, a little
girl happened to
pass by their

house. She was called Goldilocks and she was a most inquisitive child. There in front of her stood the bears' house and she just could not resist going right up to it and taking a quick peep in through the window. The first things that caught her eye were the three bowls of porridge, piping hot. They looked delicious! Goldilocks suddenly felt very, very hungry. She tiptoed round the front of the house and poked her head around the door to see if anyone was at home. Nobody was there. So she marched right into the house and the smell of steaming porridge made her feel hungrier than ever. She picked up Great Big Bear's spoon and tasted his porridge. *Ouch!* It was far too hot. So she tried Medium-sized Bear's porridge. *Ugh!* It was far too salty. Then she tried Little Tiny Bear's porridge and that was neither too hot, nor too salty. It was just right. And so Goldilocks sat down at the table and ate it all up, every single drop.

After breakfast, as Goldilocks felt rather tired, she decided to have a rest. She sat down in Great, Big Bear's chair. It was too hard. Next she tried Medium-sized Bear's chair. It was too soft. And then she sat down in Little Tiny Bear's chair. That was just right. But the porridge must have made Goldilocks too heavy for she suddenly heard a nasty cracking sound

and before she knew where she was, Goldilocks was sitting on the floor and the chair was all in pieces.

After that Goldilocks decided to explore upstairs. There in a bedroom she saw three beds, a Great Big bed, a Medium-sized bed, and a Small Tiny bed. She lay down on the Great Big bed – but that was too hard. Then she tried the Medium-sized bed, but that was too soft. So finally she tried the Tiny Little bed and that was just right. In fact it was so comfortable that Goldilocks fell fast asleep.

Just about that time the three bears decided to return home to eat their breakfast. The first thing that Great Big Bear saw was a spoon in the middle of his porridge so he called out: *"Who's been eating my porridge"* in his very loud voice. Then Medium-sized Bear saw that her porridge had been spilt and she called out: *"Who's been eating my porridge?"* Then the Little Tiny Bear looked at his bowl and all he could see was a spoon in the middle of it, with no porridge in the bowl at all so he cried: *"Who's eaten my porridge?"* and he started to cry.

Then Great Big Bear looked at his chair and saw it was all messed up so he growled: *"Who's been sitting in my chair?"* And Medium-sized Bear cried: *"Who's been sitting in my chair?"* And last of

all Little Tiny Bear looked at his chair and sobbed: *"Who's been sitting in my chair and broken it all into pieces?"*

Then the Three Bears marched up the stairs to see if they could find the culprit.

As soon as Great Big Bear looked at his bed he bellowed: *"Who's been sleeping in my bed?"* in his deep, gravelly voice.

And when Medium-Sized Bear looked at her bed she cried out: *"Who's been sleeping in my bed?"*

And Little Tiny Bear stopped crying just long enough to point to his bed: *"Who's that sleeping in my bed?"* he sniffed in his squeaky little voice.

The cries and commotion that followed woke up Goldilocks and the sight of the Three Bears standing close to her bed gave her such a fright. Without a second's hesitation she leapt out of bed and jumped straight out of the bears'

bedroom window. She might well have injured herself, for the ground she landed on was extremely hard. But Goldilocks did not stop, not even to look at her grazed hands and knees. She ran and ran and ran all the way home without turning around once to see if the Three Bears were following her. You will be glad to learn that Goldilocks arrived home safely and the Three Bears never saw her again.

The Twelve Dancing Princesses

Once upon a time there was a king who had twelve beautiful daughters. They slept in twelve beds in a single room. The king was jealous of his daughters and each night the door to their room was shut and bolted, but each morning the shoes by the princesses' beds were quite worn out. Nobody could discover why. The king declared that if any man discovered the secret of the worn-out shoes he could choose whichever princess he wanted for his wife. But whoever failed after three days would be put to death.

A king's son took up the challenge. In the evening of his arrival he was taken to the chamber next to the princesses, to keep watch. Soon he fell asleep and in the morning he found the princesses' shoes full of holes. The same thing happened the second night and again the third night. And so the king ordered the prince's head to be cut off. Other princes came but the same thing happened to all of them.

Now, by chance, an old soldier was travelling through a wood near the king's palace when he met an old woman who asked where he was going. "I do not really know," said the soldier, "but I want to discover where the princesses dance."

"Well," said the old dame, "that is no very hard task. Just don't drink any of the

wine which the princesses will give you and pretend
to fall asleep."

The old woman then gave him a cloak, saying:
"As soon as you put on that cloak you will become
invisible."

Shortly afterwards the soldier offered his services
to the king and when evening came he was led to
the outer chamber. Just as he was about to lie down,
the eldest of the princesses brought him a cup of
wine. Secretly, he threw the wine away, then
lay down on his bed and began to snore
loudly. At once all the princesses got out of
bed and dressed in front of
the mirror. As they were

dressing the youngest said: "I don't know why it is; you are all so happy, yet I feel uneasy."

"You simpleton," said the eldest, "you are always afraid. Have you forgotten how many kings' sons we have tricked? As for this soldier, even without our sleeping potion he would have slept soundly."

The eldest princess then clapped her hands. Instantly a trap door flew open and her bed dropped into the floor. The soldier watched as they stepped down one after another. The soldier jumped up, put on the old woman's cloak and followed them. In the middle of the secret stairway he accidentally trod on the gown of the youngest princess, whereupon she cried out: "Help! Someone is tugging at my gown."

"You silly creature!" scolded the eldest, "it is nothing but a nail in the wall."

At the bottom of the stairs they found themselves at the entrance to a most delightful grove of trees whose leaves were of glittering silver. The soldier broke off a little branch – *snap*: "I am sure all is not right," wailed the youngest, "did you not hear that noise?"

"It is only the sound of the fairy princes shouting for joy at our approach," countered the eldest.

They came to a second grove of trees whose leaves were of gold and to a third whose leaves were of glittering diamonds. From a tree in each grove the soldier broke off a branch.

Finally they reached a great lake where twelve little boats waited with twelve handsome princes in them.

Into each boat stepped one of the sisters. The soldier joined the youngest princess and her prince and as they rowed across the lake the prince remarked: "I do not know why it is, but though I am rowing with all my might the boat feels heavy and I am quite tired."

On the other side of the lake the boats landed. In front of them stood a fine castle. Inside the castle each prince danced with his princess until dawn when their shoes were quite worn out. Then the princes rowed back over the lake and there took their leave. When the tired princesses approached the secret stairway, the soldier ran on before them and lay down on his bed.

In the morning the soldier said nothing about his discovery, but resolved to see more. He followed the princesses on the second night, and on the third night. When the time came the soldier was taken before the king who asked where his twelve daughters danced at night. The soldier answered: "With twelve princes in a castle under ground." And he showed the king the three branches.

The princesses confessed everything and the king asked which of his daughters the soldier would choose for his wife. "I am not very young, so I will have the eldest," he replied.

They were married that very day, and thus the soldier became heir to a great kingdom.

Fox
and a
Crow

One morning a fox was returning to his lair after a
night's hunting. He had not caught anything and he
was feeling very hungry. As he passed the farmer's house
he saw a crow stealing a delicious looking piece of
cheese that the farmer's wife had left in the window. His
mouth watered and he thought to himself how he could
get the crow to give him the cheese. The crow flew off
and perched far above his head in a nearby tree. The fox
ran to the foot of the tree and started flattering the crow.

"Oh, beautiful bird," said the fox, "so graceful, so delightful and so well loved by everyone. What lovely feathers you have, and how lucky you are to be able to see into the future. Truly you are possessed of all the virtues and I cannot think of any bird so blessed. However, I do not think I have ever heard you sing. If your singing is even half as good as all your other qualities, there cannot be another creature in the whole world so fabulous."

The crow was flattered by this and to show the fox that his voice was as beautiful as the rest of him he opened his beak and started singing so that the fox might hear him. But of course, as he opened his beak the cheese dropped out and the fox snapped it up and ate it in two gulps.

"Ah ha," said the fox, "I spoke of your beauty, but you will notice I said nothing about your brains."

And the moral of this story is beware of flatterers who may just be after something for themselves.

Hansel and Gretel

Once upon a time there was a woodcutter who lived with his wife and two children at the edge of the forest. He had little in the world he could call his own and he was so poor that he had scarcely enough bread for his family to eat. At night he lay on his bed, restless and full of care.

"What is to become of us?" he asked his wife. "What shall we do?"

"Listen to me," she replied. "Take the two children out early tomorrow morning and give each of them a piece of bread. Then lead them right into the middle of the wood, where it is thickest. Build up a fire for them, and go away and leave them alone, for we can no longer keep them here."

"No, wife," said the husband, "I cannot leave my children to the wild beasts of the forest. They would soon tear the poor things to pieces."

"Oh! What a fool you are!" answered the wife. "In that case we must all starve together." And she

nagged him and nagged him
until he agreed at last to
carry out her plan.
Meanwhile the children,
lying awake in bed,
overheard everything that
their father and stepmother had said. "Now we are
abandoned," thought Gretel, and she began to weep. But
Hansel crept to her bedside, and said: "Do not be afraid,
Gretel, I will find an answer."
He got out of bed and went outside into the cold night. The
moon shone brightly on the white pebbles in the little
courtyard in front of the cottage. Hansel put as many
pebbles as he could into his pocket, and returned to the
house. Soon he fell fast asleep.
Early in the morning, before the sun had risen, the
woodman's wife came and woke them up: "Get up
children," she said, "we have to go into the wood. I
have a piece of bread for you but take care of it and
keep some for the afternoon."
After they had walked for a while, Hansel stood still
and looked back towards their home and a little
later he turned to look again, and then again,
until his father said: "Hansel, why do you keep
turning and lagging behind so?"
"I am stopping to look at my white cat that
sits on the roof and wants to say good-bye
to me," answered Hansel.

"You little fool," said his stepmother, "that is not your cat; it is the morning sun shining on the chimney-top." Now Hansel was really staying behind to drop one white pebble after another along the road. When they came to the middle of the wood their father said: "Run about children, gather up some wood and I will make a fire to keep us warm." So they piled up a little heap of brushwood, and set it on fire and as the flames burned bright their stepmother said: "Now, settle by the fire, and go to sleep while we cut wood in the forest. Be sure to wait there till we come and fetch you."

Hansel and Gretel sat by the fireside until late afternoon. They believed their father was still in the wood, because they thought they could hear the blows of his axe. But the noise was that of a bough which he had hung on a tree, and as the wind blew it backwards and forwards against the other boughs it sounded like the strokes of an axe.

When it was quite dark and no one came to fetch them, Gretel began to cry but Hansel said: "Wait, Gretel, till the moon rises." And when the moon rose he took her by the hand, and showed her the pebbles along the ground glittering like new pieces of money and marking out the way.

Towards morning they arrived at the woodman's house, and he was glad in his heart when he saw them again,

for he hated leaving
them alone. His wife also
seemed to be glad, but inwardly she
was angry and burned with rage.
Not long afterwards when they were
again almost without bread Hansel and
Gretel heard their stepmother say to her
husband: "The children found their way
back once but now there is only half a loaf of
bread left for them in the house. Tomorrow
you must take them deeper into the wood and
lose them completely, or we shall all starve."
The woodman did not dare to disagree with
his selfish wife. When the children heard their
plan, Hansel decided to gather up pebbles
again, but that night when he tried to open
the door he found his stepmother had locked
and bolted it. But he comforted Gretel, and
said: "Sleep in peace, dear Gretel! God is very
kind, and will help us."
Early in the morning a piece of bread was
given to each of the children, and while they
were walking through the woods Hansel
crumbled his piece in his pocket and
scattered crumbs on the ground.
"Why do you lag behind, Hansel?" asked
the woodman, "be on your way."
"I am looking at my little dove, sitting
upon the roof, who wants to say
good-bye to me," replied Hansel.
"You silly boy!" said the wife, "that is
not your little dove; it is the morning
sun that shines on the chimney-top."
But Hansel still went on crumbling
his bread, and throwing it on
the ground. And thus
they advanced

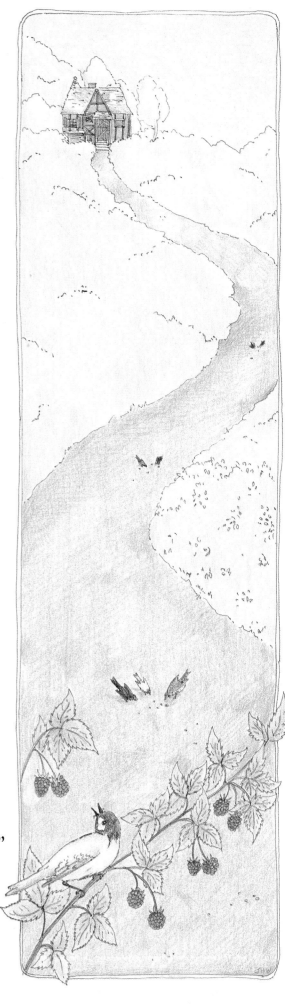

further and further into the wood, to a part they had never seen before in all their lives.

The woodman and his wife built a large fire and said they would come in the evening and take them home. The children waited and waited but no one came. "Wait till the moon rises," said Hansel, "I shall then be able to see the bread which I scattered and it will show us the way home." At last the moon rose, but when Hansel looked for the crumbs they were gone, for hundreds of little birds in the wood had found them and picked them up. The children were soon lost in the dark wilderness. All night long and all the next day they wandered about, till at last they lay down and fell asleep.

The next afternoon, when they were fainting with hunger, they came to a strange little hut. It was made of bread, with a roof of cake, and windows of candy sticks. "Now, at last, we can sit down and eat till we have had enough," said Hansel. "I will eat the roof and you, Gretel, can eat the windows."

But while Gretel was picking at the candy sticks, a shrill voice from within:

"Nibble, nibble, little mouse,
Who's nibbling my house?"

The children answered:

"The wind, the wind,
That blows through the air."

Next, Gretel broke out a pane of the window, and Hansel tore off a large piece of cake from the room, but just as they were starting to eat the door opened and a wizened old lady hobbled out. Hansel and Gretel were so frightened that they let fall what they had in their hands. But the old lady nodded to them, and said, "Dear children, where have you been wandering? Come inside with me and you shall have something good."

So she took them both by the hand and led them into her little hut, and brought out plenty to eat, milk and sugared pancakes, apples, and nuts. Then two beautiful little beds were got ready, and Gretel and Hansel laid themselves down, and thought they were in heaven.

But in fact the old lady was a spiteful witch who used her pretty candy house as a trap for children. Early in the morning, before they were awake, she snatched up

Hansel and shut him up in a pen in the stable. The witch next shook Gretel, calling out: "Get up, you lazy little thing, fetch some water and go into the kitchen and cook something good to eat. Your brother is shut up all ready for fattening, and when he is fat enough I shall eat him." So the best food was cooked for poor Hansel while Gretel got nothing but crab-shells. Every morning the old witch hobbled out to the stable and cried: "Hansel, put out your finger, that I may feel if you are getting fat." But Hansel always stretched out a bone, and the old woman, whose eyes were dim, couldn't see it, and thinking always it was Hansel's finger, wondered why he fattened so slowly.

After six months of this she finally lost patience. "Gretel," she squawked at the girl, "quick, get some water. Hansel may be fat or thin but I shall kill him tomorrow and cook him." "First of all we'll bake," the witch cackled. "I've heated the oven already and kneaded the dough."

"Creep in," said the witch

as she pushed Gretel towards the oven, "and see if it's properly heated, so that we can bake the bread." Gretel hesitated: "I don't know how I'm to do it. How do I get in?"

"You silly goose!" retorted the witch, "that opening is big enough. See, I could get in myself." She crawled towards the oven and poked her head into its dark opening.

At once Gretel gave her a tremendous shove and pushed her right in. She then slammed shut the door, and drew the iron bolt. How the witch yelled, it was quite horrible; but Gretel did not stay. She ran straight to Hansel, opened the stable door, and cried: "Hansel, we are free, the old witch is dead." How they rejoiced and jumped for joy! And as they no longer had cause for fear, they entered the old hag's house. There they found boxes and caskets stuffed with all kinds of pearls and precious stones. "These are even better than pebbles," said Hansel, and crammed his pockets full of them. "Now," said Gretel, "we must escape from the witch's wood."

At last, the wood started to look more and more familiar and soon, in the distance, they saw their father's house. Then they set off to run home and, bounding through the open door, fell into the arms of their father.

The woodcutter had not passed a single happy hour since he had left his children in the wood and his wife, had fallen ill and died. In great excitement, Gretel shook out her apron. The pearls and precious stones rolled about the room, and Hansel threw down one handful after another from his pockets. Their troubles were at last over and the woodcutter and his children lived happily ever after.

Jack the Giant-Killer

Once upon a time, in the reign of King Arthur, there lived a wealthy farmer with a son called Jack. In the neighboring county, Mount Macally, there lived a huge and monstrous giant who terrified the local townsfolk. At his approach they would abandon their homes and the giant would seize their cattle, carrying half-a-dozen oxen on his back at a time. As for their sheep and hogs, he would tie them round his waist like a bunch of bananas. Soon the whole area was devastated by his raids.

One day Jack asked the town councillors what reward would be offered to any person destroying the giant. "We would give him the giant's treasure," they said.

"Then I will destroy him," replied Jack.

So he furnished himself with a horn, a shovel, and a pickaxe, and crossed over to the Mount one dark winter's evening. There he fell to work, and before sunrise he had dug a deep pit which he covered over with long sticks and straw. At the break of day, Jack put the horn to his mouth, and blew *"Tantivy"*, *"Tantivy"*. This aroused the giant, who rushed from his cave, crying: "You villain, have you come here to disturb my rest? I will take you whole and broil you for breakfast." No sooner had the giant uttered the words than he tumbled headlong into the pit, which shook the very foundations of the Mount.

Then Jack took his pickaxe and gave the giant a most weighty knock on the very crown of his head, and killed him instantly.

When the local dignitaries heard of his deeds, they declared that Jack should henceforth be given the title, "Jack the Giant-Killer," and they presented him with a sword and an embroidered belt, on which were written these words in letters of gold:

> *"Here stands our brave and valiant man,*
> *Who slew the giant Cormelian."*

The news of Jack's victory soon spread over all the country and a giant, by name of Blunderbore, vowed revenge. Now Jack, some time later, was walking near the very wood inhabited by this giant. Tired and weary, he sat down to rest by the side of a pleasant fountain and soon fell fast asleep. There Blunderbore discovered him, and recognizing Jack, by the lines written on his embroidered belt, he hoisted him onto his shoulders and carried him towards his enchanted castle. The giant locked Jack in an immense chamber full of bones, and went off to fetch a neighbouring giant to share in the boy's destruction. While he was gone, Jack heard a magic voice crying:

> *"Do what you can to get away,*
> *Or you'll become the giant's prey."*

In the corner of the room lay four strong cords. Jack grabbed two of the cords and made a strong noose at the end of each. His window overlooked the castle gate and, as the giants returned, he cast out the ropes, landing one noose over each of their heads. Then, drawing the ends across a beam, he tied them tightly together. Quickly he slid down one of the ropes and as he came face to face with the giants, Jack drew his sword and slew them both. Jack took the giant's keys, unlocked the castle doors and released all the prisoners. He then resumed his journey.

As night fell he came to a large house. He knocked at the gate and there was a monstrous giant with two heads. The giant welcomed Jack jovially and offered him a bed for the night. But in the dead of night Jack heard the giant muttering:

> *"Though here you lodge with me this night,*
> *You shall not see the morning light."*

"So that's what you think," said Jack. He leapt out of bed, stuffed a pillow in his place and hid in a corner of the room. At the dead time

of night in came the giant. He struck several blows on the bed with his club, confident that he had broken every bone in Jack's body. The next morning he was amazed when Jack appeared. "How have you rested?" asked the giant; "did you not feel anything in the night?"

"No," replied Jack, "nothing but a rat, which swished her tail over me two or three times, I believe."

"You must have some breakfast," growled the giant. And he brought Jack a bowl containing four gallons of cold porridge.

"I will trick this wicked giant," thought Jack.

He put a large leather bag under his coat and tipped the porridge into it. Then, telling the giant he had a trick to show him, he took a knife, ripped open the bag, and out poured all the cold porridge. The challenge was too great for the giant to resist.

"Odds splutters, I can do that trick myself!" The monster snatched up a knife, ripped open his belly, and fell down dead.

Now, it happened at that time that King Arthur's only son decided to travel to a neighboring country to rescue a beautiful lady possessed with seven evil spirits. After several days' travel, the prince came to a market-town where he learned that a man had just been arrested for stealing bread. "Let him free," he urged the townsfolk, "this money shall help you to replace the loaf and, indeed, will leave you with money in hand."

Jack who was passing that way was so taken with the generosity of the prince that he asked if he might be his servant. And so the next morning the two men set forth on their journey together. As they rode out of town, an old woman called after the prince: "He owed me two coins these seven years; pray pay me as well as the rest." Putting his hand to his pocket, the prince gave the woman all he had left.

When the sun began to set, the King's son turned to Jack: "Since we now have no money, where shall we lodge this night?"

"Master, we'll do well enough, for I have an uncle lives within two miles of this place; he is a huge and monstrous giant with three heads; I myself will go ahead and prepare the way for you."

Jack rode away full speed and, coming to the gate of the castle, he

knocked with all his might. The giant roared out like thunder: "Who's there?"

"Only your Cousin Jack with bad news, I fear."

"Listen," replied the giant, "I am the giant with three heads, and I can fight five hundred men in armor, and make them flee away as fast as the driven snow,"

"No, uncle, the king's son is on his way with a thousand men in armor to kill you and destroy everything that you have."

"Oh, Cousin Jack," said the giant, "this is bad news indeed. I will hide. Lock, bolt, and bar me in, and keep the keys until the prince is gone." Jack locked up the giant and then fetched his master. That night while the poor giant lay trembling in a vault under the ground, the prince and Jack ate and slept in peace.

Early in the morning Jack sent the prince on in advance while he freed the giant from the vault. The giant asked Jack how he might reward him for keeping the castle from destruction.

"Why" said Jack, "I really want nothing but the old coat and cap, together with the old rusty sword and slippers which are at the head of your bed."

"Take them all," said the giant. "The coat will keep you invisible, the cap will furnish you with knowledge, the sword will cut to pieces whatever you strike. And the shoes are of extraordinary swiftness."

Jack thanked his uncle and left the castle. Soon he had caught up with the prince and the two men traveled to the house of the enchanted lady. She prepared a splendid banquet but as they finished eating she wiped the prince's mouth with a handkerchief and said: "Show me that handkerchief tomorrow or else you'll lose your head."

In the middle of the night she called upon her evil spirits to carry the handkerchief away but Jack put on his coat of darkness and his shoes of swiftness and followed the evil one to his lair. Jack seized the handkerchief and brought it back to his master, who in the morning showed it to the lady. The next night the same thing happened and she called again to the evil spirit, angry with him for letting the handkerchief go. Jack, the invisible, did not hesitate. He cut off the devil's head and brought it to his master, who the next morning presented it to the lady. Thus the enchantment was broken and the evil spirits left her. Now she appeared in all her beauty and the prince and his lady decided to get married. They returned to the court of King Arthur, where Jack, for his many great exploits, was made a Knight of the Round Table.

Beauty and The Beast

Once upon a time a rich merchant lived in great splendor with his sons and daughters. One day they were struck by terrible misfortune for their house caught fire and, at the same time, the merchant's fleet was destroyed. All that was left to them was a small wooden house in the middle of a dark forest.

After two years, the merchant received news that one of his ships had come safely into port and he set off immediately to claim his cargo. His children were overjoyed and they begged him to bring them back jewels and fine clothes; only the youngest child, called Beauty, did not ask for anything.

"And what shall I bring you, Beauty?"

"There is nothing that I need," she answered.

"But, Beauty, I must bring you something," her father insisted.

She laughed: "Then perhaps you could bring me one single rose."

But when the merchant reached the seaport he found that the report was false. There was no cargo and in great distress he started

the long journey home. Deep
snow and bitter frost hindered his
progress and at night, cold and exhausted, he crouched
in the hollow of a tree and listened to the howling of
wolves. When day broke, his path had become covered
by snow. He was lost.

After many hours the snow suddenly vanished
without warning and the merchant found himself in a
beautiful avenue of orange trees, leading to a most
splendid palace. He walked slowly towards it and
climbed a flight of marble steps.

Inside the palace he passed through
several splendidly furnished rooms
but everywhere he went a deep silence
reigned. At last the merchant found
a small room and there lay down on a
couch in front of a blazing fire. Soon, tired
out, he fell asleep. When he awoke he
saw, close to the couch, a little table
covered with delicious food. He ate in
silence and then wandered back through the
rooms and into the surrounding gardens.

Out in the walled garden the sun shone,
the birds sang, and the flowers bloomed. He
stopped and picked one single red rose for
Beauty but as he did so he heard a strange
rumbling noise. He turned and found
himself face to face with a frightful, angry
Beast.

"Who told you that you might gather my
roses?" the Beast called out in his deep,

echoing voice. "I have sheltered you and fed you. Why do your steal my flowers?" "Pardon me, noble sir," replied the merchant. Then he told the Beast the whole story of his ill fortune.

"I will spare your life on one condition," replied the Beast. "You must bring one of your daughters to live with me."

"But how can I do such a thing?" protested the merchant.

"I give you a month to return with one of your daughters and she must come willingly. Do not imagine that you can hide from me, for if you fail to keep your word I will come and fetch you."

The following day the merchant set out on his journey, riding a white horse given to him by the Beast. When he reached home he presented Beauty with her rose and then told his children all that had happened.

"I am the cause of this misfortune," Beauty said, "for I asked you to pick the rose. I will be the one to return to the castle with you."

One month later, mounted on the back of the white horse, Beauty returned to the palace with her father. There they went straight to the little room where a splendid fire was burning and the table was daintily spread with food. When they had finished their meal they heard the Beast approaching and as he entered the room Beauty struggled to hide her feelings.

"Have you come willingly?" asked the Beast, in a voice that would have struck terror into the boldest heart. Beauty answered bravely that she had indeed come of her own free will.

"I am pleased with you," said the Beast, "as for you, old man," he added, "at sunrise you will take your departure. You will find the white horse waiting to take you home." Then, turning to Beauty, he said: "Take your father into the next room and help him to choose gifts and treasures for your brothers and sisters."

The following morning two horses were waiting, one loaded with treasure. The merchant mounted the first horse and as he turned to say goodbye the horses galloped away at such speed that Beauty lost sight of her father almost instantly.

She wandered sadly back to her own room, and lay down to rest. As she slept she dreamed that she was walking by a brook, overhung with myrtle trees, lamenting her sad fate. There by the stream a most handsome prince

approached her.

"Ah, Beauty! try to find me, no matter how I may be disguised. I love you dearly. In making me happy you will find your own happiness."

"What can I do to make you happy?" replied Beauty.

"Only be grateful," he answered, "and do not trust too much to your eyes."

When Beauty awoke she set out to explore the palace. The first room she entered was lined with mirrors, and Beauty could see herself reflected on every side. In one mirror she caught sight of a bracelet hanging from a chandelier. To her great surprise she found that it held a portrait of the Prince who had appeared in her dream. She slipped the bracelet onto her arm and flung open the doors leading to the next room, a gallery hung with splendid pictures. Immediately she was drawn towards a portrait of the same handsome prince. Beauty then explored a room containing every musical instrument imaginable and after, when she grew tired of playing and singing, she opened a door leading to a vast library. So many books! It would take her a lifetime to read them. As darkness fell, wax candles in candlesticks of diamonds and rubies lit up the library and Beauty returned to her room.

In silence she ate the meal prepared for her but, as she finished, she heard the Beast's footsteps approaching. He greeted her in his gruff, deep voice and Beauty told him how she had passed the day. When he got up to leave he asked: "Do you love me, Beauty? Will you marry me? Do not fear to say 'yes' or 'no'."

"Oh no, Beast," said Beauty hastily, quite taken aback.

That night Beauty dreamed once more of her unknown prince. Why was she so unkind to him, he asked her. Her dream merged into another dream, then another, but in each one her charming prince was present.

The following morning Beauty decided to amuse herself in the garden, for the sun was shining and the cool fountains were playing. Everything was strangely familiar to her and in her wanderings she came to the brook where the myrtle trees grew and where she had first met the prince in her dream.

Each day Beauty made new discoveries; a room full of silks and ribbons one day, an aviary of rare birds the next. Best of all, a room with magic windows where, before her eyes, a pantomime was acted out, with dances and colored lights and music.

Every evening after supper the Beast came to visit her and asked her to marry him. Each evening she refused his offer.

After a time Beauty began to long for the company of her father and her brothers and sisters and she asked the Beast if

she might visit them. He sighed mournfully but
nevertheless agreed to let her go for two months:
"Return when your time is up or you will have cause to
repent. If you do not come your faithful Beast will be dead."

When Beauty awoke the next morning she was in an oddly
familiar room. She rushed out to greet her father and to hug her
brothers and sisters. Beauty was overjoyed to be with her family but
she often found her thoughts returning to the Beast. Two months
passed by but her family could not bear to let her go. One night she
had a most dismal dream in which she wandered along a lonely path
in the palace gardens. She heard terrible groans and found the Beast
stretched out upon his side, apparently dying.

The following day she announced to her family that she must
return to the palace. That night she turned her ring round and
round upon her finger, as instructed, and said in a clear voice: "I
wish to go back to my palace and see my Beast again." She fell asleep
instantly and awoke in the palace.

But in the evening the Beast failed to appear and Beauty was
terrified. Up and down the paths and avenues she ran, calling in
vain, until at last she stopped for a minute's rest and found herself
standing opposite a shady path. Hurrying down the path she came
to a cave in which lay the Beast, asleep, so Beauty thought. She
approached and stroked his head, but he did not move. She ran to
fetch some water which she sprinkled over his face. As he began to
revive she cried: "Oh, Beast, how your frightened me! I never knew
how much I cared for you until I feared I was too late to save your
life."

"Beauty, you came only just in time. I was dying because I
thought you had forgotten your promise. Go back now to the palace
and I shall meet you there."

Beauty returned to the palace and when the Beast came he asked,
as he had so often before: "Beauty, will you marry me?" This time
she answered softly: "Yes, dear Beast." As she spoke a blaze of light
lit up the windows of the palace; fireworks crackled and guns fired
and across the avenue of orange-trees, in letters made of fireflies,

were the words: "Long live the prince and his bride."

Turning to ask the Beast what was the meaning of all this, Beauty found that, in his place, there stood the prince of her dreams! At the same moment the wheels of a chariot clattered on the terrace and two ladies entered the room. One turned to Beauty: "How can I thank you enough for rescuing my son from this terrible enchantment." And then she tenderly embraced the prince and Beauty.

The marriage was celebrated the very next day with the utmost splendor, and Beauty and the prince lived happily ever after.

Snow-white and Rose-red

Once upon a time there was a poor widow who lived in a little cottage with her two children, Snow-white and Rose-red. The two sisters loved each other dearly and they were the sweetest and best children in the whole world.

Snow-white and Rose-red often roamed alone through the woods gathering berries, feeding animals and birds: the little rabbit would nibble at a cabbage leaf from their hands, and the birds would sing to them. One evening they decided to sleep in the woods, and when it grew dark they lay down together and fell into a deep sleep.

In the morning, just as the sun rose in the sky, they saw, standing close by, a child dressed in a shimmering white robe. The child smiled sweetly at them but spoke not a word before he vanished into the wood. Snow-white and Rose-red were frightened – for they realized that they had been sleeping close to the edge of a great cliff.

When they returned home they told their mother about the child and the cliff. She smiled: "The angel who looks after good children has been watching over you."

One winter evening there was a knock at the door. Rose-red drew back the bolt and there, standing in the darkness, was a poor, dishevelled man. Yet this was no man – it was a bear who poked his thick brown head around the door. Rose-red screamed aloud and sprang back in terror. Immediately the bear began to reassure her: "Don't be afraid, I won't hurt you. I am half-frozen and only wish to warm myself a little."

"Poor bear," said the mother, "lie down by the fire." The bear asked the children to beat the snow from his fur, and they scrubbed him until he was dry. Then he stretched himself in front of the fire.

The children loved playing with the big brown bear, they tugged at his fur, plonked their feet on his back, and rolled him about hither and thither. When it was bedtime the mother turned to the bear and said: "You can stay here and take shelter."

In the morning, when the children unbolted the door, the bear trotted out of the house and back into the wood. But from that day onwards, the bear came every evening at the same hour and played with the children, then lay down by the hearth.

When spring came and all outside was green, the bear said: "Now I must go away and leave you for the summer."

"Don't go, dear bear. Why must you leave us?" asked Snow-white.

"I need to protect my treasure for wicked dwarfs desire to steal it. In winter, when the earth is frozen hard, they stay underground. But now the sun has warmed the earth, they reappear and steal anything that is precious." Snow-white and Rose-red were sad. They said good-bye and Snow-white unbolted the door. As she did so, the bear caught a piece of his fur in the door-knocker and Snow-white thought she spied the sparkle of glittering gold beneath his fur.

One spring day, the mother sent her children out to gather sticks for the fire. In a clearing in the wood, they came upon a big tree trunk

stretched right across their path. There, in the long grass they saw a
squat dwarf with a wizened face and a long flowing beard. The end of
his beard was jammed into a cleft of the tree, and the little man was
tugging hard, like a dog on a chain. He glared at the girls with his fiery
red eyes and screamed out: "What are you doing you ninnies? Can't you
help me?"

"What's the matter, little man?" asked Rose-red innocently.

"You stupid, inquisitive goose!" replied the dwarf, "I was trying to split
this log but the wood was so slippery my wedge fell out of the cleft; I am
stuck fast by my beard." The children pulled and pulled but it was no
good.

"I've got just the thing," said Snow-white as she took out her scissors
and snipped off the end of his beard. "You horrid wretches, cutting off a
piece of my splendid beard. What cheek!" muttered the dwarf as he
seized a bag full of gold hidden in the grass, and disappeared.

A few days later Snow-white and Rose-red went to the stream to catch
some fish. When they got there they saw an enormous grasshopper
spring toward the water. They ran forward eagerly but whom should it
turn out to be but that wizened old dwarf. "Where are you off to?" asked
Rose-red, "you're surely not going to jump into the water?"

"I'm not such a fool," screamed the dwarf. "Can't you see that that fish is trying to pull me in?"

The dwarf had hooked a big fish and his long beard had got caught up in his line. The girls held him firm and tried to help but they could not free him and so out came the scissors and snip. "You toadstools!" he yelled. "How dare you disfigure me so. I can't appear like this. You horrid interfering little girls!" He stormed off to the nearby rushes, snatched up a sack of pearls and disappeared.

Soon after this Snow-white and Rose-red went to the market town to buy some ribbons and lace. As they were walking along, they saw a great bird slowly circling above them. Suddenly the bird swooped down and pounced on something hidden behind a rock. There was a sharp cry. The children ran forward and there, caught in the talons of the eagle, was the nasty little dwarf. They grabbed his coat and pulled and pulled and finally the eagle let go.

"Treat me more carefully!" screeched the ungrateful fellow. "You have torn my clothes to pieces, you good-for-nothings." And he picked up a bag of gold and vanished under a rock. On their way home Snow-white and Rose-red met the dwarf once more. He was crouched over a mound of dazzling jewels. The children could hardly take their eyes off them. "What are you standing gaping at my stones for?" screamed the dwarf, scarlet with rage. But he was interrupted by a deep

growling noise and a big, brown bear ran out from behind a rock.

"Dear bear!" whined the evil dwarf, "Spare me, spare me. Take all my treasure and look, eat up these two wicked girls – tasty morsels I'd say."

The bear paid no attention but struck the dwarf one mighty blow with his paw and the wizened creature never moved again. The girls fled in terror but the bear called after them: "Snow-white, Rose-red, don't be afraid. Wait." They recognized the bear's voice and as he came towards them the bear's fur fell off and before them they saw a handsome prince all dressed in cloth of gold.

"I am a king's son," he told the girls, "doomed to wander the woods as a bear until I could catch and kill that evil dwarf, when the curse would be lifted and I would be myself again."

Snow-white married the prince and Rose-red his brother and between them they divided the great treasure. The mother came to live with her children and in the garden she planted two rose trees, one white and one red.

The Tinder Box

Once upon a time there was a soldier who came marching along the highway. One, two! One, two! He had been to the wars and he was on his way home. On the road he met an old witch; she was so ugly her lower lip hung right down to her chin. "Good evening soldier!" she said. "What a nice sword you've got and such a big knapsack. You're a real soldier. You shall have as much money as you wish."

"Thank you, old witch," answered the soldier.

"See that big tree," said the witch, "it is

hollow inside! Climb up
and you will see a hole going right down
under the tree! Let yourself down and I will
haul you up again when you call."

"What for?" asked the soldier.

"To fetch money!" said the witch. "When you
get down to the bottom of the tree you will find
a wide passage with three doors. Go into the first
room and you will find a big box in the middle of the
floor. A dog is sitting on top of it, and he has eyes as
big as saucers. Spread my blue-checked apron out
on the floor; pick up the dog, put him on it, open
the box and take out as much money as you like. It
is all copper, but if you like silver, go into the next
room. There you will find a dog with eyes as big as
millstones. Put him on my apron and take the
money. If you prefer gold you can have it too, and
as much as you can carry. The gold is in the box in
the third room. But the dog
sitting on that box has eyes as
big as the Round Tower. He
is a dog indeed. But don't
let it trouble you. Just put
him on my apron and then
he won't hurt you, and
you can take as much
gold out of the box as
you like!"

"That's easy enough,"
said the soldier, "but
what am I to give you
old witch, for you'll

want something."

"No," said the witch, "not a single penny. I only want you to bring up the old tinder box that my grandmother forgot last time she was down there!"

"In that case, tie a rope round my waist," said the soldier. "Here you are," said the witch, "and here is my checked apron." Then the soldier climbed up the tree, let himself slide down the hollow trunk, and found himself in the wide passage where many hundreds of lamps were burning. He opened the first door. Ugh! There sat the dog with eyes as big as saucers staring at him.

"You're a nice fellow," said the soldier, as he put him on the witch's apron, and he took as many pennies as he could cram in his pockets. Then he shut the box, put the dog back on top of it again, and went into the next room. There sat the dog with eyes as big as millstones. He put that dog on the apron but when he saw all the silver in the box he threw away the coppers and stuffed his pockets and his knapsack with silver. Then he went into the third room. Oh! how horrible! That dog really had eyes as big as the Round Tower, eyes that rolled round and round like wheels.

"Good evening, dog," said the soldier saluting.

Then he lifted the dog down onto the apron and opened the chest. What a pile of gold! he could buy the whole city with it, and all the sugar-pigs from the

cake women, and all the rocking-horses in the world!

So the soldier threw away the silver and put gold in its place. He crammed his pockets with so much gold he could hardly walk! He put the dog back on the box, shut the door, and shouted up the tree: "Haul me up, you old witch!"

"Have you got the tinder box?"

"Oh! to be sure," said the soldier. "I had quite forgotten it." And he went back to fetch it. Then the witch hauled him up, and there he was standing on the high road with his pockets, boots, knapsack and cap, full of gold.

"What do you want the tinder box for?" asked the soldier.

"Mind you own business," said the witch. "You've got the money, give it to me!"

"No!" said the soldier. "Tell me directly what you want with it, or I will draw my sword and cut off your head."

"I won't!" said the witch.

So the soldier cut off her head – there she lay dead! The soldier then tied all the money up in her apron, put the tinder box in his pocket, and marched off to the town.

It was a beautiful town, and he went to the finest hotel, ordered the grandest rooms and all the food he liked best. Next day he bought new boots and splendid clothes, and became a fine gentleman. The people told him all about the grand things in their town, and about their king and the lovely princess, his daughter.

"Where can I see her?" asked the soldier. "You can't see her at all," they replied, "she lives in a great copper castle surrounded with walls. Nobody but the king goes in and out, for it has been foretold that she will marry a soldier, and the king doesn't like that." The soldier now led a merry life. He went to the theatres, drove about in the park, and gave away money to the poor. He wore fine clothes, and had many friends.

But as he went on spending money every day he soon found himself with only two coins left. He had to move out of his fine rooms. He took a tiny attic up many stairs and none of his friends ever came to see him. One dark evening when he had not even enough money to buy a candle, he suddenly remembered that there was a small candle in the old tinder box he had brought out of the hollow tree. He got out the tinder box and struck fire, but, as the sparks flew out from the flint, the door burst open and the dog with eyes as big as saucers stood before him and said: "What does my lord command?" "By heaven," said the soldier, "this is a nice kind of tinder box. Get me some money." The dog vanished and was back in a twinkling with a big bag full of pennies in its mouth. Now the soldier found what a treasure he had in the tinder box. If he struck once, the dog which sat on the box of copper came; if he struck twice, the dog on the silver box came; and if he struck three times, the dog guarding the box of gold came. He moved back to his grand rooms with all his fine clothes and all his friends came back to see him.

Suddenly, he began to think. It was a curious thing that no man could ever see the princess. What was the good of her beauty if she was always shut up in that copper palace. The soldier struck the flint, and, *whisk*, came the dog with eyes as big as saucers. "I know that it is the middle of the night," said the soldier," but I am very anxious to see the princess if

only for a moment."
The dog was out of the door in an instant, and before the soldier had time to think, he returned with the princess. There she was, fast asleep on the dog's back, and she was so lovely that anyone could see that she was a real princess. The soldier kissed her for he was a true soldier.
Then the dog ran back with the princess, but in the morning, when the king and queen were having breakfast, the princess said she had had a wonderful dream about a dog and a soldier. She had ridden on the dog's back and the soldier had kissed her.
"That's a pretty tale," said the queen, but she made an old lady in waiting sit by her daughter's bed that night.
The soldier longed to see the princess again and the next night he sent the dog to fetch her. But, when the dog appeared, the lady in waiting ran behind them and she made a big cross on the gate of the soldier's house. When the dog took the princess back to the palace he saw the cross and he made crosses on all the gates in the town.
When the queen heard about all this she determined she would discover what

was happening. She made a pretty little bag of silk, which she filled with wheat. She stitched it to the princess's nightgown and she cut a small hole in it so that the grains would drop out to show where the princess went.

The dog never noticed the grains and the next morning when the king and queen saw where the trail had finished they seized the soldier and commanded that he be thrown into the dungeons. There he lay for months. Then one day they said to him: "Tomorrow you will be hanged."

That morning he could see through the bars of his cell window the people hurrying out of town to see him hanged. Everyone was going; among them was a shoemaker's boy in his leather apron and slippers. He was in such a hurry that he lost one of his slippers, and it fell under the soldier's window. "I say, you boy! Don't be in such a hurry," said the soldier to him. "Nothing will happen until I get there. But if you run to the house where I live, and fetch me my tinder box, I will give you a gold coin!"

The boy tore off, got the tinder box and gave it to the soldier.

Now – outside the town a high scaffold had been erected, surrounded by crowds of people. The king and queen sat on a throne opposite the judges and councillors. The soldier mounted the scaffold but just as they were putting the rope around his neck he asked the king whether he could, as one final favor on earth, smoke one last pipe. The king could not deny him this, so the soldier took out his tinder box and struck fire, once, twice, three times, and there were all the dogs. The one with eyes like saucers, the one with eyes like millstones, and the one with eyes as big as the Round Tower.

"Help me! Save me from being hanged!" cried the soldier. So the dogs rushed at the hangman and the guards and the councillors, and they took one by his legs, and one by his nose, and they threw them up so high in the air that when they came down they were all broken into small pieces.

"No!" cried the king as the biggest dog seized him and the queen at the same time. But the dog just tossed them in the air.

Then everyone shouted: "Good soldier, save us! You shall be our king and marry the princess."

So the soldier was conducted to the king's chariot and the three dogs danced in front of him shouting "Hurrah!". The boys all whistled and the soldiers presented arms. The princess came out of the copper palace and she became queen and that pleased her very much. The wedding took place that week and all the dogs

came and sat at a special table with their
eyes staring and going round and round.

The Three Little Pigs

Once upon a time there were three little pigs who went out into the world to seek their fortune and build their own houses.

The first little pig met a man carrying a bundle of straw: "Please, man, give me some straw to build me a house," he asked. The man gave him some straw, and the little pig built his house. Presently along came a wolf who knocked loudly at the door and called: "Little pig, little pig, let me come in."

And the little pig squealed: "No, no, by the hair of my chinny, chin chin!"

The wolf replied: "Then I'll huff and I'll puff and I'll blow your house in."

So he huffed, and he puffed, and he blew the house in, and gobbled up that little pig.

The second little pig jogged along and met a man carrying a bundle of wood: "Please man, give me some wood to build me a house," and the man gave him some wood, and the little pig built his house.

Then along came the wolf, who

called out: "Little pig, little pig, let me come in."

"No, no, by the hair of my chinny, chin chin," squealed this little pig.

"Then I'll puff, and I'll huff, and I'll blow your house in."

So he huffed, and he puffed, and he blew the wooden house down, and gobbled up the second pig.

The third little pig met a man carrying a load of bricks: "Please, man, give me those bricks to build me a house." So the man gave him the bricks, and this pig built a fine house. Presently the wolf came along and said: "Little pig, little pig, let me come in."

"No, no, by the hair of my chinny chin chin."

"Then I'll huff, and I'll puff, and I'll blow your house in."

Well, he huffed, and he puffed, and he puffed and he huffed, but he could NOT blow the brick house down. The wolf then decided to trick the little pig so he said: "Little pig, I know where there is a nice field of turnips."

"Where?" asked this little pig.

"Oh, in Farmer Smith's field, and tomorrow morning we will go together and get some of these turnips for dinner."

"Very well," said the little pig, "What time do you intend to set off?" "Six o'clock is turnip-picking time," replied the wolf. But this little pig got up at five o'clock and gathered the turnips before the wolf came. When the wolf arrived he called out: "Little pig, are you ready?"

"Ready!" exclaimed the little pig, "I have been and come back again, and got myself a nice potful for dinner, thank you."

The wolf was very angry, but he still believed that he could trick the little pig. "Little Pig, I know where there is a nice apple tree," he said. "Where?" said the pig.

"Down at Merry Orchard," replied the wolf, "I will come for you at five o'clock in the morning."

The little pig set out at four o'clock in the morning, hoping to get back before the wolf's visit. But the journey was long, and he also had to climb the apple tree. Just as he was scrambling down he spied the wolf who jumped up at the tree and snarled: "Little pig, I see that you are here before me. Tell me, are those apples tasty?"

"Extremely tasty," the little pig assured him, "I will throw one down for you so you can taste one for yourself." He threw the apple right down the hill so, while the wolf was chasing it, the little pig jumped down and ran home safely. The next day the wolf came again, and said to the little pig: "Little pig, there is a fair in the town this afternoon. Will you go?" "Oh, yes," said the little pig, "certainly. What time will you be ready?"

"At three o'clock precisely," said the wolf. So the little pig went off at two o'clock and bought a butter-churn at the fair. Just as he was heading for home with the churn he spied the wolf. The little pig scrambled into the churn, and rolled down the hill inside it. The wolf was terrified by the churn and ran all the way home without even stopping to visit the fair. When he returned to the little pig's house, the little pig laughed at him. "Ha! Ha! You were really frightened. It was me inside that butter churn, rumbling and rolling down the hill."

The wolf was white with rage. He sprang onto the roof to get down the chimney. But the pig had a large pot boiling on the fire and as the wolf came down he took off the lid and – SPLASH – in fell the wolf. The little pig popped on the cover again, boiled up the wolf, and ate him for supper. And, of course, this little pig lived happily ever after.

The Frogs Choose

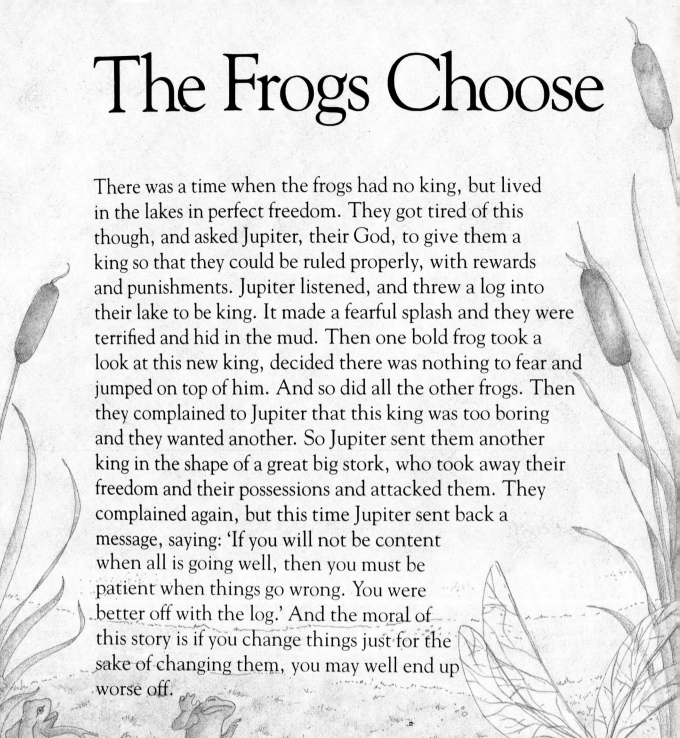

There was a time when the frogs had no king, but lived
in the lakes in perfect freedom. They got tired of this
though, and asked Jupiter, their God, to give them a
king so that they could be ruled properly, with rewards
and punishments. Jupiter listened, and threw a log into
their lake to be king. It made a fearful splash and they were
terrified and hid in the mud. Then one bold frog took a
look at this new king, decided there was nothing to fear and
jumped on top of him. And so did all the other frogs. Then
they complained to Jupiter that this king was too boring
and they wanted another. So Jupiter sent them another
king in the shape of a great big stork, who took away their
freedom and their possessions and attacked them. They
complained again, but this time Jupiter sent back a
message, saying: 'If you will not be content
when all is going well, then you must be
patient when things go wrong. You were
better off with the log.' And the moral of
this story is if you change things just for the
sake of changing them, you may well end up
worse off.

a King